Pony Trouble

Dale Blackwell Gasque

ILLUSTRATED BY STACEY SCHUETT

Hyperion Books for Children

New York

To Courtney and Kate—
the best of cousins
—D. B. G.

Printed in the United States of America

First Edition
1 3 5 7 9 10 8 6 4 2

The artwork for this book is prepared using gouache.
The text for this book is set in 16-point Berkeley Book.

Library of Congress Cataloging-in-Publication Data
Gasque, Dale Blackwell.
Pony Trouble / Dale Blackwell Gasque; illustrated by Stacey Schuett.— 1st ed.
p.   cm.
Summary: Amy envies her cousin Rebecca's skill at gymnastics and swimming, not
knowing that Rebecca wishes she had Amy's way with animals.
ISBN 0-7868-1218-4 (pbk.)—ISBN 0-7868-2267-8 (lib. bdg.)
[1. Cousins—Fiction. 2. Horses—Fiction. 3. Self-confidence—Fiction.] I. Schuett,
Stacey, ill. II.Title.
PZ7.G2145Co   1998
[Fic}—dc21   97-18047

CONTENTS

CHAPTER 1

Problem Pony

Wait up," Amy shouted, jamming her foot into her sneaker. But her cousin Rebecca was already out of the car and running toward the pasture.

"*Agggh.*" Amy blew the hair off her forehead as she struggled with a knot.

By the time Amy caught up, Rebecca was standing on the bottom fence-board calling to the ponies. Her blond hair was a lot longer than it was last summer. It swished like a horse's tail. All of a sudden Amy wished her

plain brown hair was long enough for a ponytail, too, even though it was too curly to be smooth and silky like Rebecca's.

"Is that one mine?" Rebecca asked. "She's so cute."

"You mean *he*. Taffy will be very insulted if you call him a girl."

Rebecca pretended to slap herself, then fell off the fence into a backward somersault. Amy giggled. She was glad her cousin had come to Vermont to visit for a week.

"I have a horse model that looks just like him," Rebecca said, climbing back up. "What do you call horses that are that color?"

"Palomino," Amy answered as she watched the ponies eat grass. Taffy's body was the color of a caramel apple, but his mane and tail were as light as Rebecca's hair. Amy's parents had borrowed him for Rebecca's visit. Lightning, the bigger pony, belonged to Amy. He was white with splashes of black and chocolate brown, like caramel turtle fudge ice cream.

"And Lightning is a pinto." Amy was pleased to know something Rebecca didn't. Even though she was ten now and Rebecca wouldn't be ten until September, it sometimes seemed like her cousin was better at everything—except riding. But ever since Rebecca wrote from Maryland about jumping two feet at her riding lessons last winter, Amy worried that Rebecca might beat her in riding, too.

"Come on," she said, handing Rebecca a halter and lead rope. "Let's catch them."

By the time she closed the gate, Rebecca was racing ahead. The ponies stopped eating grass and watched.

"Don't run," Amy warned, but it was too late. The ponies trotted to the far corner of the field. "You can't run up on ponies like that," she said. "Hide the halter behind your back and hold the carrot out like this."

Lightning was easy to catch. He pushed his brown nose into the halter and munched his carrot. Amy stood on tiptoe to fasten the buckle. "Good boy," she said, patting his neck.

Rebecca was having trouble. Taffy would watch out of the corner of his eye as he ate grass, moving away just as she got ready to pounce. "Stupid pony," she yelled, slipping in the tall grass.

Amy laughed when Taffy looked back and swished his tail. "He's not stupid. You just need to make friends with him."

Rebecca kept trying to catch Taffy, but the pony was playing keep-away. He tossed his head as he trotted out of Rebecca's reach.

Amy got tired of waiting. "Come on, Lightning," she said, tying the lead rope on both sides of his halter. She used a big rock to help her climb on him bareback.

"Stay there," she told Rebecca. "Let me try something." Amy squeezed Lightning with her legs and steered him toward Taffy. When they were side by side, she slid off and put her arms around Taffy's golden neck.

"Bring the halter," she said. "But don't run."

Amy had to help get the halter on because Rebecca couldn't do up the buckle. "Don't you do this stuff at your riding lessons?"

Rebecca shook her head. "The horses are saddled when we get there. I'd rather have more time to ride, anyway," she added with a shrug. "Can I take Lightning? He's better trained."

Amy pretended not to hear her as she gave Lightning a tug and began walking toward the barn. She remembered how bossy Rebecca could be. As soon as Amy and Lightning reached the gate, Rebecca screamed.

"*OWWWWW! Get off!*"

Amy turned and saw Rebecca hitting Taffy's shoulder. By the time Amy ran back, he had moved off Rebecca's foot.

"You okay?" Amy asked, feeling a little guilty when she saw Rebecca's tears. Well, it wasn't her fault Rebecca got stepped on, she reasoned. Sometimes Lightning stomped on her toes, too.

"Dumb pony did it on purpose," Rebecca said with a sniff, giving Taffy's lead rope a jerk. The pony stepped back, his eyes wide with alarm.

That made Amy mad. Who did Rebecca think she was, blaming Taffy for everything? "You have to keep your feet away from his hooves," she said.

"I tried." Rebecca had dirt on her face where she rubbed her eyes.

Amy sighed and looked toward the house. She knew what Mom would say. "Okay. I'll lead Taffy, and you can lead Lightning."

CHAPTER 2

Cousin Trouble

It is *so* cool having my own pony to ride." Rebecca hopped and did a perfect cartwheel in the grass.

"Come on," Amy said. Sometimes Rebecca was a real show-off.

They had put the ponies in the barn while they ran to the house to change into their riding clothes. Mom was going to give them a lesson.

"You're lucky to live on a farm," Rebecca said, skipping down the hill and into the big red barn.

Amy thought so, too, but she didn't want to brag. "It's a lot of work. I have to help feed the horses and clean their stalls, even when the snow is too deep to ride."

Rebecca took a deep breath and twirled in the aisle. "Horses and sawdust are my favorite smells in the whole world."

"Mine, too," Amy said, smiling. "Come on. I'll help you get ready."

When both ponies were brushed and saddled, Amy held Taffy so Rebecca could get on. Her cousin looked like a show rider in her new breeches and boots. Amy sighed as she looked down at her jeans and hiking shoes. Riding clothes cost too much.

"I ride bigger horses than Taffy at my riding lessons," Rebecca said.

Amy put her left foot in the stirrup and gave a little hop, swinging her leg over Lightning's back and landing softly in the saddle. "I like ponies," she said, leaning forward to pet his silky neck. "If Lightning were any bigger, I wouldn't be able to tack up and get on by myself."

On the way up the hill to the fenced ring, Taffy kept stopping to eat grass. "I can't get this stupid pony's head up." Rebecca's face was red from tugging on the reins.

"It might help if you stopped calling him stupid," Amy muttered under her breath. "Squeeze him forward and pull on the reins at the same time," she said louder. "It's easier to get his head up when he's walking."

It worked, but Rebecca still looked annoyed.

"It'll be okay when we get to the ring," Amy said. "There's no grass, and even Taffy wouldn't try to eat sand." That made Rebecca laugh.

As soon as they closed the gate, Rebecca started trotting. She should walk longer to warm up first, Amy thought with disapproval. She didn't say anything, though, until Rebecca started kicking Taffy with her heels to make him canter. Taffy just trotted faster.

"You better wait for Mom," Amy warned as they raced around the corner. Rebecca was posting so high out of the saddle, she was almost standing in her stirrups.

One minute Rebecca was going up and down like a sewing machine needle, and the next minute she was tipping to the inside like she was leaning off a merry-go-round. When she screamed, Taffy jumped to one side and left her in the sand.

"Are you all right?" Amy said as she trotted over, hoping Rebecca wasn't hurt.

Rebecca hardly looked at her as she stood up. "Bucked me off," she said, brushing at her legs. "Now my new pants are dirty."

Serves you right for showing off, Amy thought as she went to catch Taffy. The pony was on the edge of the ring reaching under the fence to nibble grass. Amy laughed when she saw the saddle hanging upside down under his belly. "Poor Taffy."

"Poor Taffy?" Rebecca said. "You mean poor me."

Amy shook her head. "The saddle slipped because the girth wasn't tight enough. You should always check it after you get on and walk a little to make sure it's still snug." Didn't her fancy riding stable teach her anything?

Rebecca stuck out her chin. "The saddle slipped because he bucked. Stupid pony."

Amy was getting sick and tired of Rebecca. "Taffy is not a stupid pony. You're the one who's stupid if you are going to blame him for everything. And for your information, Taffy didn't buck. He just moved sideways so he wouldn't step on you." Rebecca might look like a hotshot rider, but she didn't even know how to saddle a horse.

Rebecca's cheeks were red as she walked over to Taffy and without saying a word fixed the saddle.

By the time Mom came outside, Rebecca was back on. The cousins were not speaking.

CHAPTER 3

Rebecca the Perfect

I wasn't laughing *at* you," Amy said. The lesson was over and the girls were putting the ponies away. "I laughed because Taffy looked so funny with his saddle upside down."

Rebecca didn't say anything.

"I'm sorry," Amy said, wishing Rebecca would stop being mad.

Rebecca gave Taffy a pat. "Okay," she said, but didn't sound very friendly.

* * *

At dinner Rebecca sat next to Amy's four-
year-old brother, Ben. "Want me to do that?"
she asked as he tried to cut his pork chop.

"Thanks, Rebecca," Mom said. "You'll
make a good baby-sitter some day."

"I'm baby-sitting for my next door
neighbor now." Rebecca pushed Ben's plate
back.

Amy's eyes widened. "All by yourself?"

"Well, actually I'm a mother's helper. I
go over to play with the little girl next door

while her mother cleans the house or works in the garden," Rebecca explained. "I get $1.50 an hour."

Amy wished she got $1.50 an hour to play with Ben.

"So, how was school this year?" Dad asked as he passed the bread to Rebecca.

"It was fun. My class put on *The Wizard of Oz*."

"Did you have a part?"

Rebecca grinned. "I was Dorothy."

It figures, Amy thought.

"You must have a good voice to get the leading role," Dad said.

"And a good memory to learn all those lines," Mom added.

Amy was sick of hearing how good at everything Rebecca was. "Can I have dessert?"

"You *may* have dessert when the rest of us are finished," Mom said.

"Amy didn't eat her peas," Ben complained.

She stuck her tongue out at him, but Mom frowned and shook her head. Tattle-tale, Amy thought as she slumped in her chair.

* * *

When Amy finished her bath, Rebecca was lying on the bottom bunk with her back to the door reading one of the fat books she had brought. "You want to play cards?" Amy asked. She was good at cards. She bet she could beat Rebecca.

"No, thanks," Rebecca said. "I feel like reading."

Amy sighed. This visit wasn't going at all the way she planned. She flipped through the books on her shelf. Nothing looked interesting. She was glad when her guinea pig, Cleo, whistled.

"Oh, I'm sorry. I forgot your carrot." Amy ran down to the refrigerator. As she came back up the stairs, she heard a sharp squeak.

Amy rushed into the bedroom and found

Rebecca holding Cleo. She gave Amy a guilty look and put Cleo back into the cage.

"You have to be careful," Amy said. "It hurts Cleo's stomach when you pick her up with one hand."

Rebecca turned pink. "Well, *excuse* me for not being a know-it-all like you."

"I don't mind if you hold her," Amy said, her face growing hot. Rebecca was taking everything the wrong way.

"You act like you're the only one who knows anything about animals." Rebecca's eyes were squinty. "Just because you have a lot of pets and I don't, you always rub it in."

That wasn't fair. She never bragged the way Rebecca did. "*You're* the know-it-all." Amy was so mad her voice was all quivery. "Only you don't know anything. The reason Cleo squeaked is because she's going to have babies, and you have to pick her up with two hands so you don't press her stomach too hard." She folded her arms across her chest so Rebecca wouldn't see her shaking.

Cleo's whistle broke the heavy silence. *Stop that yelling!* her bright black eyes seemed to say.

Rebecca was the first to crack up. Amy laughed, too.

"Here," she said, handing Rebecca the carrot. "You give it to her." Amy put one hand under Cleo's stomach and the other hand under her bottom as she lifted the guinea pig into Rebecca's arms.

Rebecca cradled her like a doll. "When is she going to have her babies?"

"Soon, I think," Amy said. "Maybe this week."

"I wish my mom would let me have a guinea pig." Rebecca stroked the top of Cleo's head with one finger.

"I'd give you one of the babies if I could," Amy said, trying extra hard to be nice. "But even if she had them this week, they wouldn't be able to leave Cleo for a month."

Rebecca put her cheek against Cleo's shiny coat. "Mom doesn't want any animals."

Amy raised her eyebrows. Rebecca had everything: swimming pool, tree house, computer, even her own television. And Rebecca got to take gymnastics, piano, and horseback riding. Amy was only allowed to take lessons in one thing at a time because they were expensive. But Rebecca's family had plenty of money. "Why not?"

Rebecca shrugged. "She says she doesn't have time to take care of one more thing.

Being a doctor is really hard work," she added.

"But you could take care of a guinea pig yourself. All you have to do is feed it in the morning and at night and change the shavings once a week. It's simple."

Rebecca carefully sat on the bed with Cleo. When she looked up, she was smiling. "I'm going to ask Mom and Dad if I can have a guinea pig, too. They can see how neat Cleo is when they pick me up."

Amy fell back on the bed, relieved that she and Rebecca were getting along again. "I bet Cleo will have her babies by then. When your mom sees how cute guinea pigs are, she won't be able to say no."

CHAPTER 4

Even-Steven

Lightning and Taffy pricked their ears and broke into a jig as the girls rode up the driveway the next morning. Amy was glad Mom let them go on the trail. "I'd better be first," she said as they crossed the road and turned into the woods.

"Let's take turns," Rebecca suggested, sounding like a teacher. "You go first on this trail, and I'll go first on the jumping trail."

Amy didn't want to go second, but she also didn't want to fight. "Okay, but if Taffy doesn't go fast enough to stay ahead of Lightning, we'd better switch places again." She shortened her reins. "Let's trot."

They wound through the trails, ducking low branches and breathing the Christmasy smell of pine trees. "Let's go faster," Rebecca called from behind.

Amy squeezed her legs, and Lightning broke into a canter. Next they galloped up the hill and around a bend in the trail before Amy sat back in the saddle, slowing Lightning to a trot.

"Watch out," Rebecca cried. Lightning pinned his ears back and jumped sideways into the bushes as Taffy brushed by.

"Whoa," Amy said as Lightning's hindquarters swung into a tree. He shot forward onto the trail again. By the time Amy stopped him, her heart was racing. "You're supposed to keep at least one horse's length between us. You're lucky Lightning didn't kick you when you bumped into him like that."

"You should have warned me you were going to slow down," Rebecca pointed out.

She was right, but Amy didn't feel like admitting it. "Well, stay further away next time."

"Is that where we turn for the jumping trail?" Rebecca didn't wait for an answer. "Let's go!"

Taffy was in the lead now. Even though he was smaller than Lightning, he had no problem staying ahead. Amy had to nudge

Lightning with her legs to get him to keep up.

"Tallyho," Rebecca cried as Taffy jumped the first pile of logs.

Amy pushed her heels down as Lightning approached the little jump. Sometimes he jumped higher than he needed to, and Amy didn't want to get left behind. She kept her head up as Lightning flew over the logs. Taffy and Rebecca had already jumped the fallen tree and were disappearing around the bend.

Lightning didn't want to be by himself. He galloped up the hill and jumped so high that Amy's foot slipped out of her right stirrup. *"Whoa,"* she said, but Lightning wouldn't stop. He tossed his head and pulled the reins out of Amy's fingers. She grabbed his mane to keep from falling as he jumped one log after another, trying to keep Taffy in sight.

He swerved after the last pile of brush at the top of the trail, and Amy found herself sitting on his neck instead of in the saddle.

She tried to hang on, but she was leaning too far to keep her balance. The next thing she knew she was on the ground, looking up through the leaves at patches of blue sky.

"Are you okay?"

Amy was trembling as she sat up and brushed at the twigs stuck in her hair. Lightning stood nearby, chewing on a bush.

"What happened?" Rebecca asked.

Amy limped to Lightning and stroked

his nose. Thank goodness he didn't run home without her.

"I don't know," she said when she got her breath back. "A deer or something must have scared him." She brushed at the dirt on her jeans. Why did she have to go and fall off in front of Rebecca, anyway?

"I don't see any deer," Rebecca said, looking around.

Amy rolled her eyes. "It's long gone by now. If it even was a deer," she added. "Could've been a bear."

"You're kidding."

Amy was, but when she saw Rebecca's wide eyes, she couldn't resist. "It could've been. One time the farmer next door saw a black bear go into these woods."

"I hope *we* don't see one," Rebecca said, walking Taffy closer to Lightning.

Amy grinned. "I'd better go first now."

Lightning walked a few steps off the trail as Amy mounted. *"Whoa,"* she said firmly, pulling back on the reins. "Oh, my gosh," she whispered, looking in the brush. "Rebecca!"

Nestled in the middle of a patch of ferns was a small spotted fawn. Amy thought it was asleep, but then she saw a bright eye, frozen in fear.

"Ohhhh. He looks just like Bambi," Rebecca said softly. "But he's so little. We have to help him." She started to get off Taffy.

"Wait." Amy didn't want the baby to spring up and scare the ponies. "I bet the thing Lightning shied at was the mother running off. We better leave so she can come back."

"Are you sure it was the mother?" Rebecca asked.

Amy studied the fawn. He was small— not much bigger than the stuffed dog she kept on her bed. But his coat was shiny and he looked well fed, so he couldn't be an orphan.

"I think so. Let's go ahead to the field,

and if he's still here when we come back, we'll get Mom to call someone to help."

"I wish we could pet him," Rebecca said.

Amy was tempted. "Me, too. But we better leqave him alone so his mother will come back." She took one last look at the fawn. He blended into the woodsy floor. His white spots looked like places where the sun shone through the leaves. If Lightning hadn't moved off the trail, they probably would have ridden right past him.

"Well, we're even now," Rebecca said as they rode on.

"What?" Amy asked, still full of wonder at seeing a real baby deer. Wait until she told Mom.

"I mean we've both fallen off once since I got here," Rebecca said.

Amy prickled inside. Even good riders fall off sometimes.

She didn't say much to Rebecca for the rest of the ride. And when they came back down the trail, the fawn was gone.

CHAPTER 5

Second Best

It was so hot that afternoon, Mom packed a picnic dinner to eat at the lake.

"Wow," Rebecca said as they piled out of the car.

Amy looked at the little lake with the long green hill rising up behind it. It was pretty. "There are ducks, too. Darn, I forgot to bring bread for them."

By the time the girls helped carry the picnic stuff down by the water, they were sweaty all over.

"Can we go in now?" Amy asked.

Dad waved them off with a grin. "Be sure to stick together. The lifeguard's gone for the day."

Rebecca screamed when her foot touched the water. "It's cold as ice!"

Amy made herself walk straight in. "Watch." She held her breath and plunged. *Brrrr.* After swimming a few yards underwater, she wiped her eyes. "See? Nothing to it."

Rebecca scrunched her nose, counted to three, and ducked under, too. When she came up, she was grinning. "Feels good." She looked around. "Hey, you want to swim out to the raft?"

Amy stopped smiling. She didn't like going that far. "There's nothing to do out there," she said. "Let's see if Mom brought a Frisbee."

They moved to the shallow, roped-off area so Ben could play, too. When the Frisbee went into the deep water, Rebecca jumped over the rope like a dolphin. Amy tried it, too, but the rope scraped her stomach.

"You have to push off the bottom like this." Rebecca shot out of the water and arched over the rope. "It's like diving," she said when she came up on the other side.

Amy hated diving. Whenever she tried, the water slapped her stomach.

"Uncle Stan?" Rebecca called to Amy's father. "May we swim to the raft?"

"Rebecca," Amy hissed. "I don't want to go."

"Come on, honey," Dad said as he waded through the water to Amy. "I'll be right by you."

Rebecca was way ahead as they swam in the deep water. She didn't have to stop because she could turn her head to breathe. When Amy tried to breathe like that, she got water in her mouth. She had to do a lot of dog-paddling, so she was pooped by the time she flopped onto the warm, smooth boards of the raft.

"Amy, watch." Rebecca stood on her toes and did a perfect dive, slicing through the water with hardly a ripple. Dad clapped when Rebecca reappeared.

"Nice," he said. "Why don't you give Amy some pointers?"

Amy gritted her teeth. That was the last thing she wanted.

* * *

"Rebecca's better than me at everything," Amy said when Mom tucked her in that night.

Mom looked surprised. "Like what?"

"Swimming for one," Amy said. "And gymnastics and—"

Rebecca came out of the bathroom, so Amy stopped.

"Good night, Sweetie Pie," Mom said. She leaned forward, smoothing Amy's curls back from her face. "You're number one with me."

Chapter 6

Secret Swim

It's too hot to ride," Rebecca complained as they sprawled under the apple tree the next morning. "Can your mom take us to the lake again?"

That was the last place Amy wanted to go. "She's too busy."

Rebecca sighed. "At home when it's like this, all I want to do is swim."

Swim. Amy had a brainstorm. "I know a place with a pond. We could pack a picnic and ride the ponies there."

"Too hot for boots and breeches," Rebecca said, wrinkling her nose.

"We'll ride bareback in our shorts." Amy lowered her voice. "We can even take Lightning and Taffy in to swim." She always wanted to try swimming in that pond, but her parents never let her.

"Lightning can swim?"

"Sure, all horses can," Amy said, *almost* certain she was right. They did in books.

"Don't tell my mom we're going swimming, though," Amy added. "I want it to be a surprise." She didn't want to give Mom the chance to say no.

It took a while to get ready. They filled two backpacks with peanut butter and jelly sandwiches, chocolate chip cookies, potato chips, and orange sodas. They also stuck in halters, lead ropes, and carrots for the ponies.

"Have a nice picnic," Mom said as they rode up the driveway.

"We will," Rebecca answered. Amy felt a

little guilty as she waved good-bye to Mom.

"We'd better not trot," Amy said as she waited at the top of the driveway for Rebecca to catch up. "We don't want our sodas to explode when we open them."

"Good," Rebecca said. "Taffy's slippery without a saddle."

Lightning wasn't too slippery for Amy. She loved the feel of his warm, silky back against her skin. When she was on Lightning, she felt like she could do anything.

The ponies walked side by side along the old logging road as Amy and Rebecca talked about school, riding, and just about everything. Their legs got sticky with sweat, and Rebecca kept pretending she was sliding off. Amy laughed so hard her stomach hurt. When she looked up and saw the little field with the pond right in front of them, she was almost sorry to stop.

Rebecca groaned as she jumped off. "I'm sore."

"Let's eat then," Amy said, sliding off Lightning.

They led the ponies under an apple tree by the pond, putting on their halters so they could graze. When the ponies were settled and eating, the girls dug into their lunch.

Umm. Everything tastes better outside, Amy thought as Lightning tore at the grass by her feet.

Rebecca sighed. "This is great. I wish I didn't have to leave on Saturday."

"Me, too," Amy said. It was fun when the rest of her family wasn't around fussing over Rebecca.

"Wait a minute!" Rebecca waved a potato chip in the air. "Maybe you could come back to Maryland with us for a week!"

Maryland? She couldn't imagine going that far without her parents.

"You'd be there for the Fourth of July," Rebecca said. "We go downtown to the Washington Monument to watch the fireworks. They're the best in the world. Maybe we'd even get to see the president."

Amy's family always went to a field where the volunteer firemen from town shot off big fireworks every Fourth of July. Her friends would always go, too. They'd try to catch lightning bugs as they waited for it to get dark. Then she would climb into the pickup truck with Mom, Dad, and Ben to watch the show. Amy could almost taste the buttery popcorn they'd bring along in paper bags. "I don't think I can go."

"Why not? I bet we can get your parents to let you. We can go to the Air and Space Museum one day. It will be educational." Rebecca sounded very sure of herself.

"I don't think so," Amy said, shaking her head.

Rebecca stopped chewing. "You don't want to go, do you?"

"It's just that I'm going to be pretty busy," she lied, stuffing the trash into her backpack.

"Yeah? Doing what?"

Amy pushed the sweaty hair off her forehead. "Lots of things. Come on. Let's go swimming," she said, getting up to put Lightning's bridle back on.

"You're scared," Rebecca said.

"I am not." Amy's voice came out too loud. She quickly put the bit in Lightning's mouth and slid the headstall over his ears. It only took a second to do up the

throatlatch. Then she grabbed his mane and swung up on him without even standing on a rock. Rebecca couldn't do that.

"You're scared to do anything without your parents," Rebecca said with her know-it-all smile. "You don't even go to sleep without them tucking you in."

So what if her parents kissed her goodnight when she was in bed? Suddenly Amy was tired of feeling like the stuff she did wasn't good enough. She was sick of the way Rebecca could make her feel dumb.

"Think what you want," she said, turning Lightning away. "We're going swimming."

Chapter 7

Deep Trouble

Rebecca is a jerk, Amy thought as she looked for the best place to ride into the pond. I'll be glad when she goes home.

Splash!

Lightning jumped at the noise. There were round ripples in the water by the far bank.

"What was that?" Rebecca called from beneath the apple tree. Taffy snorted, staring at the water.

Something big and black made the next

splash. "Beavers," Amy shouted. She had forgotten it was a beaver pond. Lightning's ears flicked back and forth at the next splash. Now the ripples were in the middle.

"They're slapping the water with their tails," she shouted back to Rebecca. Lightning stepped forward for a better look.

"Be careful," Rebecca called. "They might have rabies or something. You'd better get back."

Amy laughed. "Watch out, Lightning. There are killer beavers out there."

"It's not funny," Rebecca said. "Wild animals carry rabies."

"Well, I've never heard of rabid beavers," Amy said. "Coming?"

"No way."

Now who's chicken? Amy thought, walking Lightning closer to the water's edge. He hesitated as his foot made a squishing noise in the soft ground, but she kicked him on. When they reached the cattails, his front end dropped. Amy fell forward onto his neck as he struggled to keep from sinking. "Whoa," she shouted as he pitched in the mud.

He stopped, but Amy could feel him trembling underneath her. She grabbed onto his mane and waited for his next move.

Nothing happened. Amy squeezed him with her legs and Lightning raised his head, but he didn't budge. The mud was so deep that Amy couldn't even see Lightning's legs. He was stuck.

"Oh, my gosh!" Rebecca screamed.

"Quiet or you'll spook him," Amy snapped. She had to keep calm so Lightning wouldn't panic and hurt them both. "Easy, boy," she said over and over, stroking his sweaty neck. How were they going to get out?

"Should I get help?" Rebecca asked.

Amy didn't know what Lightning would do if Taffy left. His heart was already beating so hard she could feel it. "Get a lead rope and toss it to me," she called to Rebecca. "But don't hit Lightning."

He stayed still when the rope landed by him. Amy took a deep breath.

"Okay, buddy. I'm going to get off now so I can help. Ea-sy," she said as she looked at the ground around her. If she crawled, she might not sink in as much.

"Be careful." Rebecca sounded scared.

Amy slid to the right into the cattails. "Don't move, buddy," she whispered as she crawled toward the rope. Mud squished through her fingers and her knees were wet, but she only sank a few inches in the spongy ground.

"Steady," Amy said as she turned back to snap the lead rope to the ring of his bit. She didn't want him to lunge at her.

Once the rope was on, Amy had to get to solid ground where she could stand up. Then maybe she could help pull Lightning out.

But the lead rope was too short to reach. "Toss me yours, too," Amy said.

Rebecca did, and Amy tied it to the first lead, talking to Lightning as she worked. She could see white as he rolled his eyes around and whinnied to Taffy. He was scared.

Amy inched through the grass until her knees stopped making squishing noises. She stood up, the end of the rope tight in her hand.

"Okay, Lightning. Come on. You can do it," she called, pulling his head around as she gave the lead a tug. Lightning jerked

his head, snatching the rope out of her hands. Amy stood helplessly as he struggled. Could he get out now that he didn't have her extra weight?

He rocked back and reared, twisting around with a mighty lunge. Half jumping, half stumbling, he fought his way back to solid ground. When he reached the short grass, he shook and trotted to Taffy.

"All right!" Rebecca cheered. Amy's throat was too tight to say a word.

Rebecca grabbed the lead rope before it tangled up in his legs. Amy stood frozen as she stared at Lightning. He was black with mud.

"What's the matter? Are you stuck, too?"

How could Rebecca joke at a time like this? "Don't you realize Lightning could have been hurt?" Amy shouted. She rushed over and threw her arms around her pony's neck. "I'm sorry, buddy," Amy whispered into his sweaty hair. A chill went down her back. What if something was broken? She ran her hands down his legs and walked him in a circle to see if he was limping.

"Is he—all right?" Rebecca asked. She looked worried.

"I think so. Thanks for helping," Amy added, sorry now that she'd yelled.

Rebecca's eyes were wide. "You were really brave. I don't know what I would have done if Taffy had been stuck."

Amy felt more stupid than brave. What if Lightning had really gotten hurt, just because she was trying to show off?

Chapter 8

Sharing Secrets

Girls," Mom called from the house as they rode down the barn driveway. "Put the ponies away and come inside."

"Uh-oh."

"Are you going to tell her?" Rebecca looked worried, too.

"Maybe she already knows." Amy only half listened to Rebecca's chatter as she washed the mud off Lightning. She ran her hands down each leg again to check for cuts or swelling. Even though he trotted off

50

to eat grass with Taffy when Amy turned him out, she still couldn't shake the bad feeling in her stomach.

"What's up?" Amy asked as she and Rebecca came into the kitchen.

"There's something I want to—good heavens," Mom said, laughing as she looked at the girls. "You two are filthy. Especially you, Amy. What did you do, take a mud bath?"

Suddenly Amy didn't want to keep a secret from her mother. "I did something dumb."

Mom stopped smiling as she listened to

what happened. When they were finished, she put her arm around Amy.

"What were you thinking of, swimming without an adult?"

Amy shrugged. It was a bad idea, now that she knew what could happen.

"Promise you won't try anything like that again without checking with me first," Mom said. She pushed the hair back from Amy's face.

"I promise," Amy said. "I was really scared Lightning was going to get hurt."

"He may be stiff tomorrow," Mom said, "so you had better just walk when you ride. Now jump into the shower, both of you," she ordered. "And don't touch anything on the way."

Amy felt as limp as a piece of spaghetti. What a relief. Even though she'd made a mistake, Lightning was going to be fine.

Rebecca poked her as they headed upstairs. "Why did your mom want us to come inside, anyway?"

Amy stopped. "I don't know. I'll ask." She hung her head over the bannister and yelled, "Mom? What did you want us for?"

"Look in your bedroom."

Rebecca was the first one there. "I don't see anything."

Amy turned when Cleo whistled. Why was she lying like that? She took a step closer and caught her breath.

"What?" Rebecca asked.

"Cleo has babies!" Amy stared at the two balls of fur nestled against the guinea pig's side. They looked like toys.

"They're so cute," Rebecca said. "I thought that they'd be bald or something."

"Not guinea pigs. They're always born with fur." Amy tried to stroke one of the babies, but it scooted away. "Mice and hamsters are the ones that are all pink and bald-looking when they're born."

"You really know a lot about animals, don't you?"

Amy squirmed, remembering the last time Rebecca brought up her pets. "I guess so."

"You ought to be a veterinarian when you grow up. You're really good with animals."

Amy felt mixed up inside. "Well, you're so good at *everything*," she blurted.

"I am?" Rebecca looked surprised.

"Yeah, you are. Mom and Dad are always talking about how good your grades are and about the ribbons you've won for swimming and gymnastics."

Rebecca started laughing.

"What's so funny?"

It was a minute before Rebecca could talk. "*My* parents are always talking about how responsible you are with horses and looking after Ben." She rolled her eyes. "And if I have to listen one more time about how you made everyone's Christmas presents last year from scratch, I'm going to puke."

"They said that about me?" Amy couldn't help but feel a little pleased. Still, she knew how Rebecca felt. "Don't you hate the way parents are always comparing?"

"Only they don't come right out and say that I'm better at swimming or you're more responsible. They're sneakier than that," Rebecca said.

Amy laughed. "You're right. They just think that if they make a big fuss about something—like you getting straight A's—," Amy paused long enough to stick out her tongue, "—then that will make me want to get straight A's, too."

Rebecca nodded. "Exactly."

All of a sudden, Amy didn't feel jealous

anymore. So what if her cousin was good at stuff? She could do a lot of things, too.

Amy smiled at Rebecca, and Rebecca smiled back.

"Do you think you could teach me how to swing up onto Taffy like you do with Lightning?"

"Sure," Amy said. "If you'll show me how to do cartwheels."

Rebecca gave Amy a high five. "All right!"

Enjoy More Hyperion Chapter Books!

ALISON'S PUPPY

SPY IN THE SKY

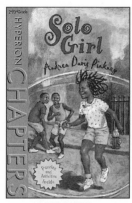

SOLO GIRL

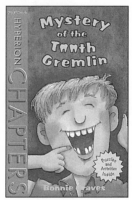

**MYSTERY OF
THE TOOTH GREMLIN**

**MY SISTER
THE SAUSAGE ROLL**

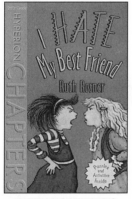

I HATE MY BEST FRIEND

**ALISON'S FIERCE AND
UGLY HALLOWEEN**

SECONDHAND STAR

GRACE THE PIRATE

Hyperion Chapters

2nd Grade
Alison's Fierce and Ugly Halloween
Alison's Puppy
Alison's Wings
The Banana Split from Outer Space
Edwin and Emily
Emily at School
The Peanut Butter Gang
Scaredy Dog
Sweets & Treats: Dessert Poems

2nd/3rd Grade
The Best, Worst Day
I Hate My Best Friend
Jenius: The Amazing Guinea Pig
Jennifer, Too
The Missing Fossil Mystery
Mystery of the Tooth Gremlin
No Copycats Allowed!
No Room for Francie
Pony Trouble
Princess Josie's Pets
Secondhand Star
Solo Girl
Spoiled Rotten

3rd Grade
Behind the Couch
Christopher Davis's Best Year Yet
Eat!
Grace the Pirate
The Kwanzaa Contest
The Lighthouse Mermaid
Mamá's Birthday Surprise
My Sister the Sausage Roll
Racetrack Robbery
Spy in the Sky
Third Grade Bullies